Just Super

Written and Illustrated by
Kimberly Mohns Roberts

www.catskillpublishing.com

ISBN 978-0-692-17495-1 (Paperback)

ISBN 978-1-7328951-0-2 (Hardcover)

Written and Illustrated by Kimberly Mohns Roberts

Digital Color by Ryan Causey

To my supporters
Thank you for believing in my mission
and sharing these important messages
with our young generation.

To my young readers
Hold tight to these lessons learned, believe in yourself,
and accept the individuality of others.

Dad?

Yes buddy?

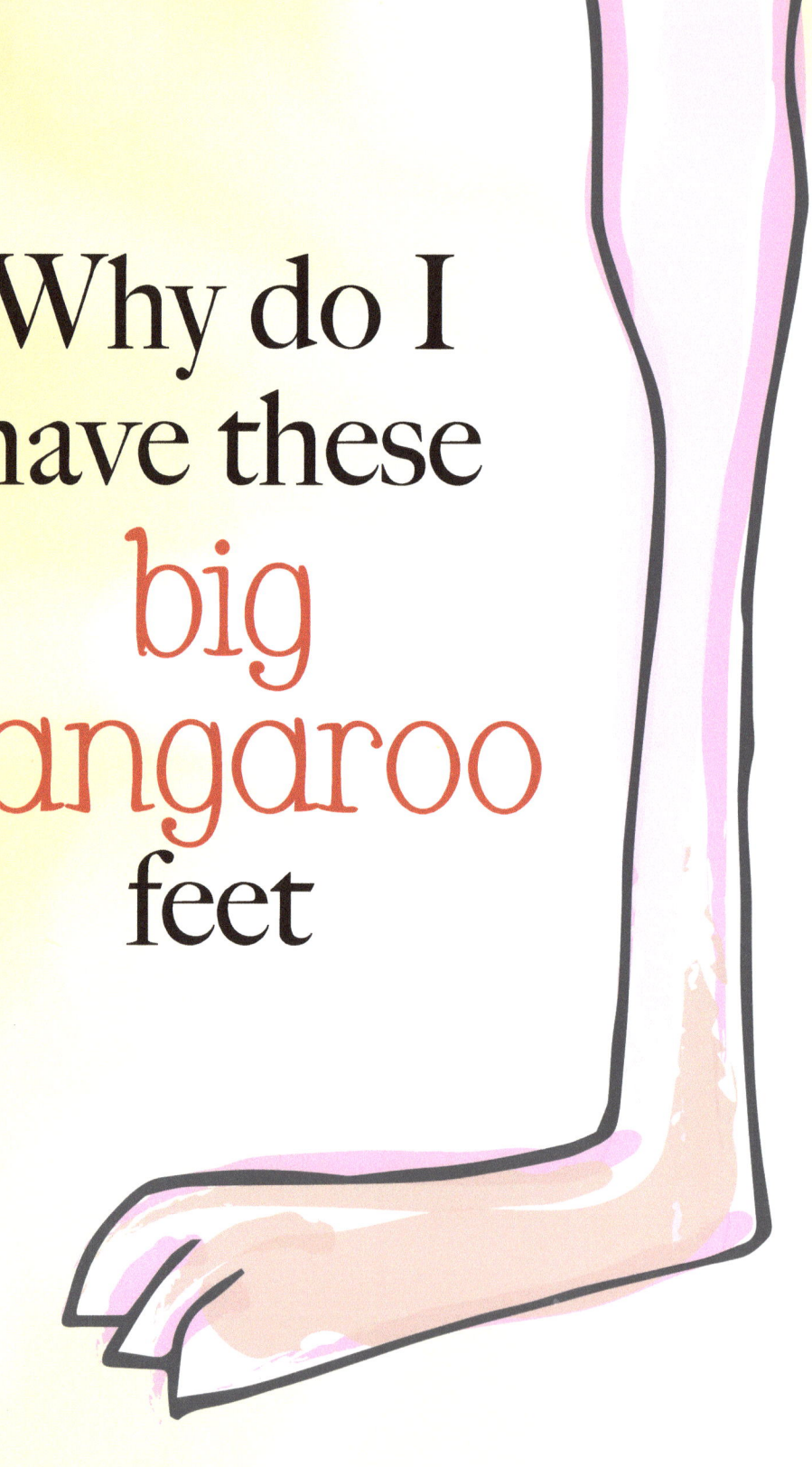

Why do I have these big kangaroo feet

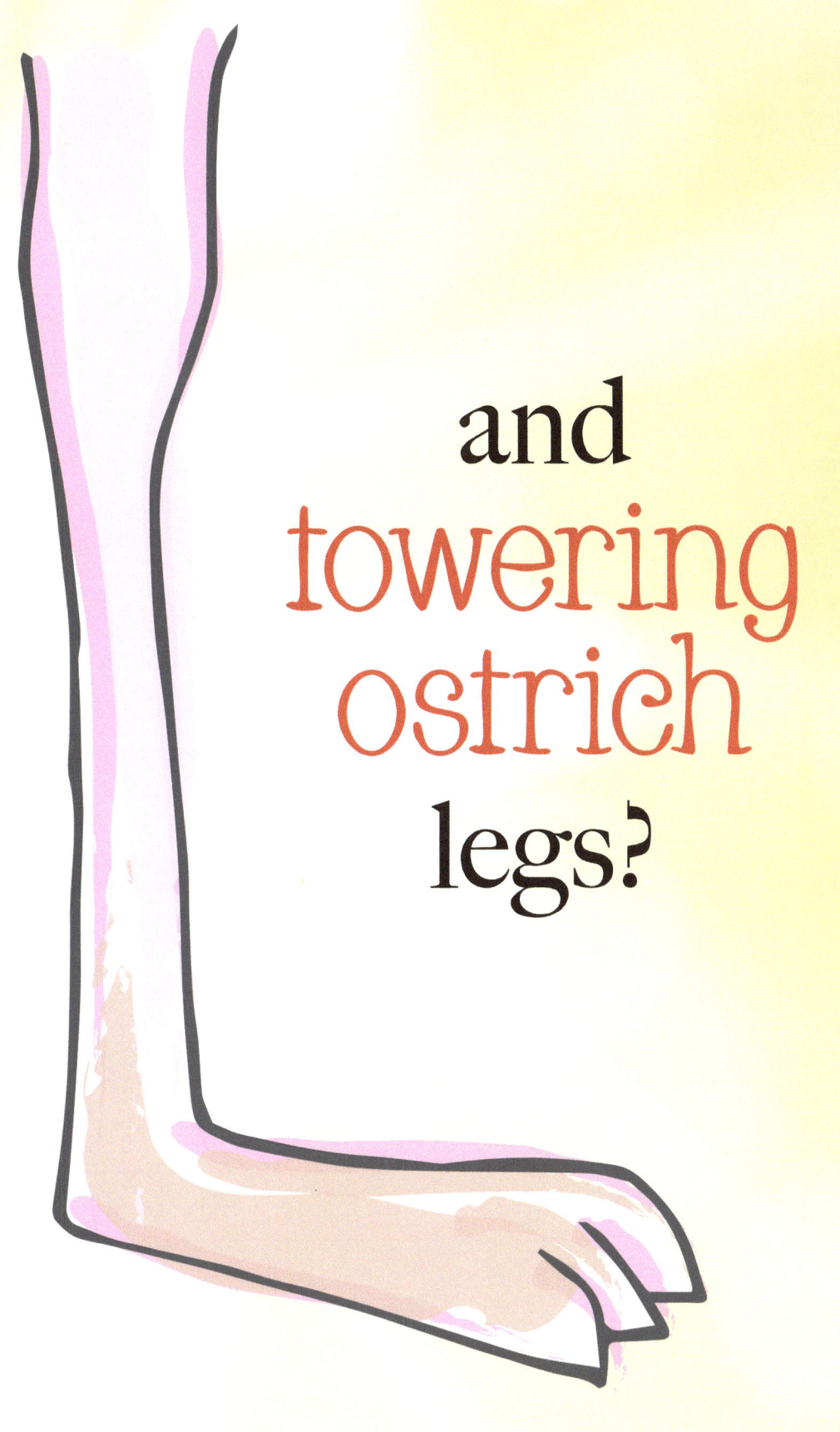

and
towering
ostrich
legs?

Tell me
about my
broad
gorilla
chest

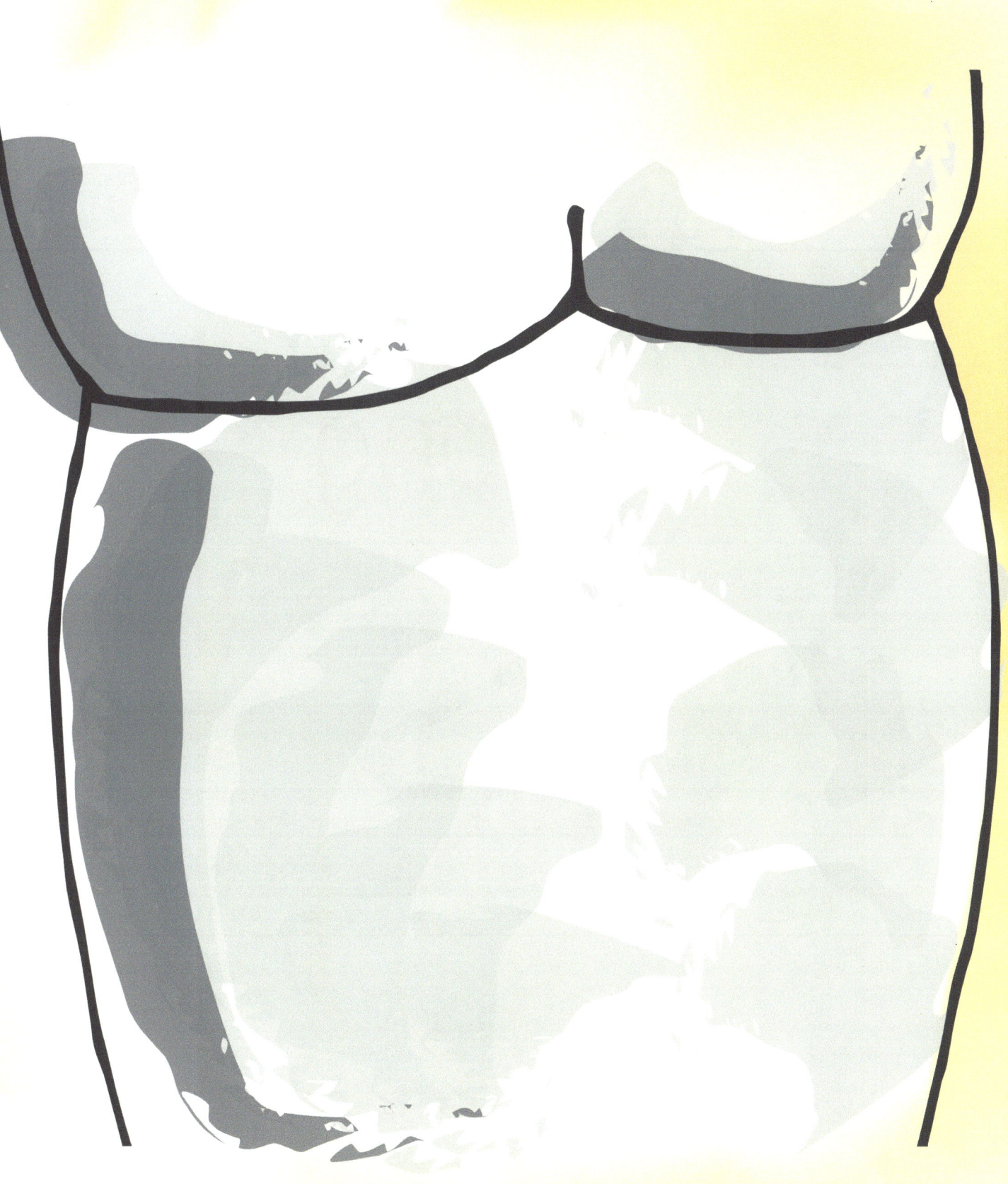

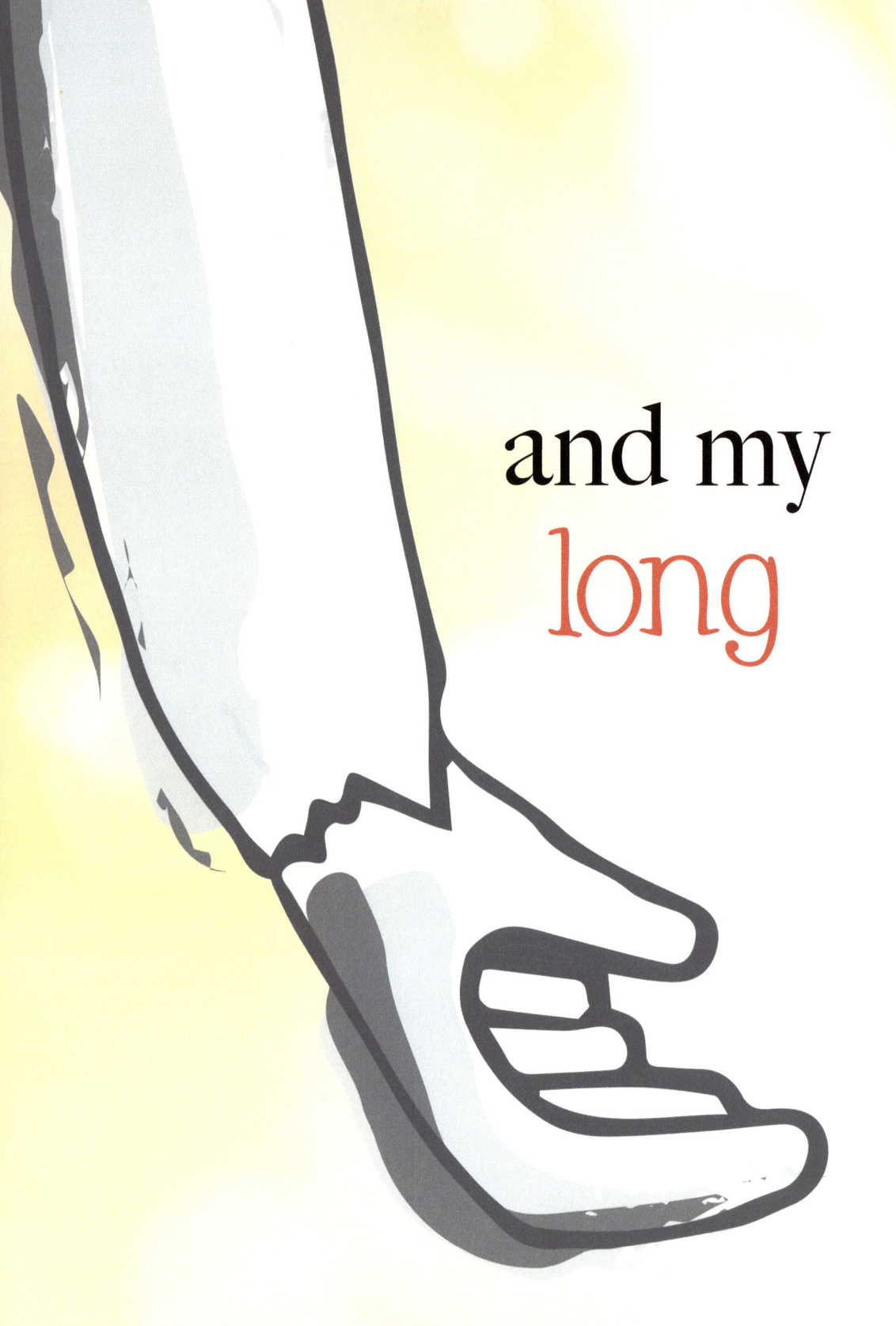

and my
long

monkey
arms?

These
large
elephant
ears seem
to get in
the way.

What
good is a
wide
hippo
mouth

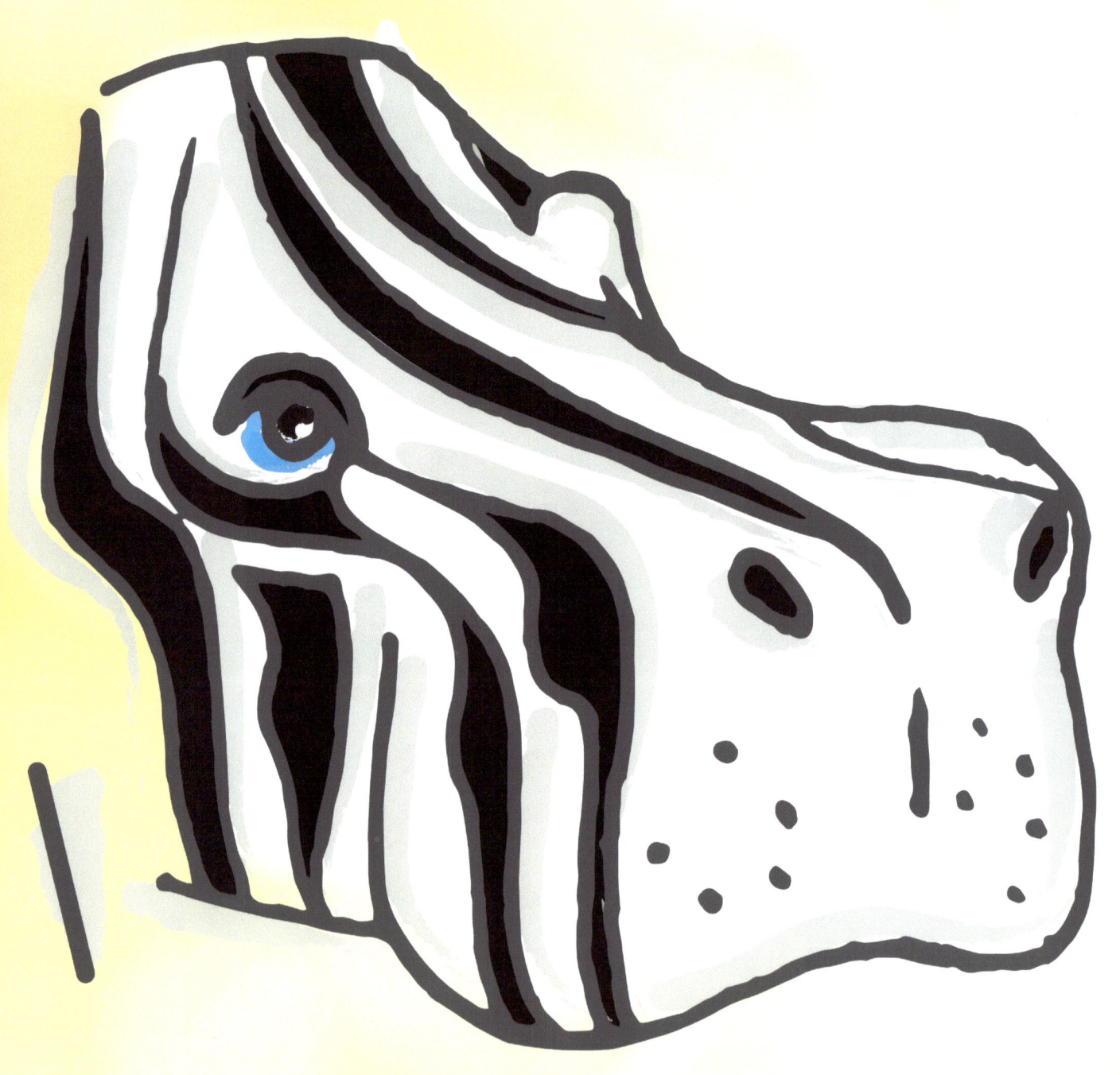

and
bold zebra
stripes?

Ah my child,

let me tell you...

Your **super kangaroo feet** keep you grounded through life's ups and downs.

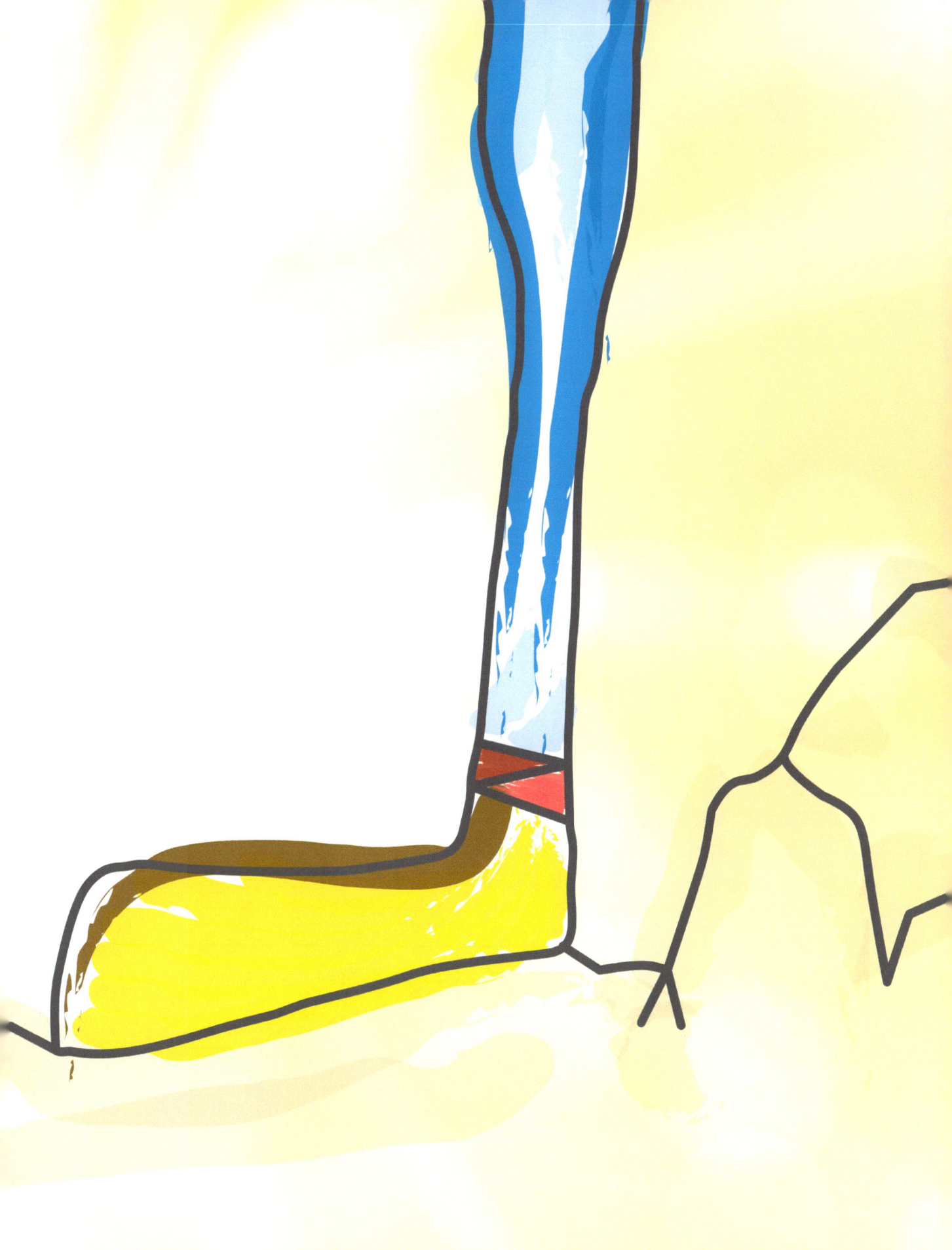

Those super ostrich legs give you a different perspective.

A

super
gorilla
chest

holds your
big heart

and those
super monkey

arms

can lift spirits.

What about those super elephant ears?

They are for listening to your conscience.

Let your voice be heard with your super hippo mouth

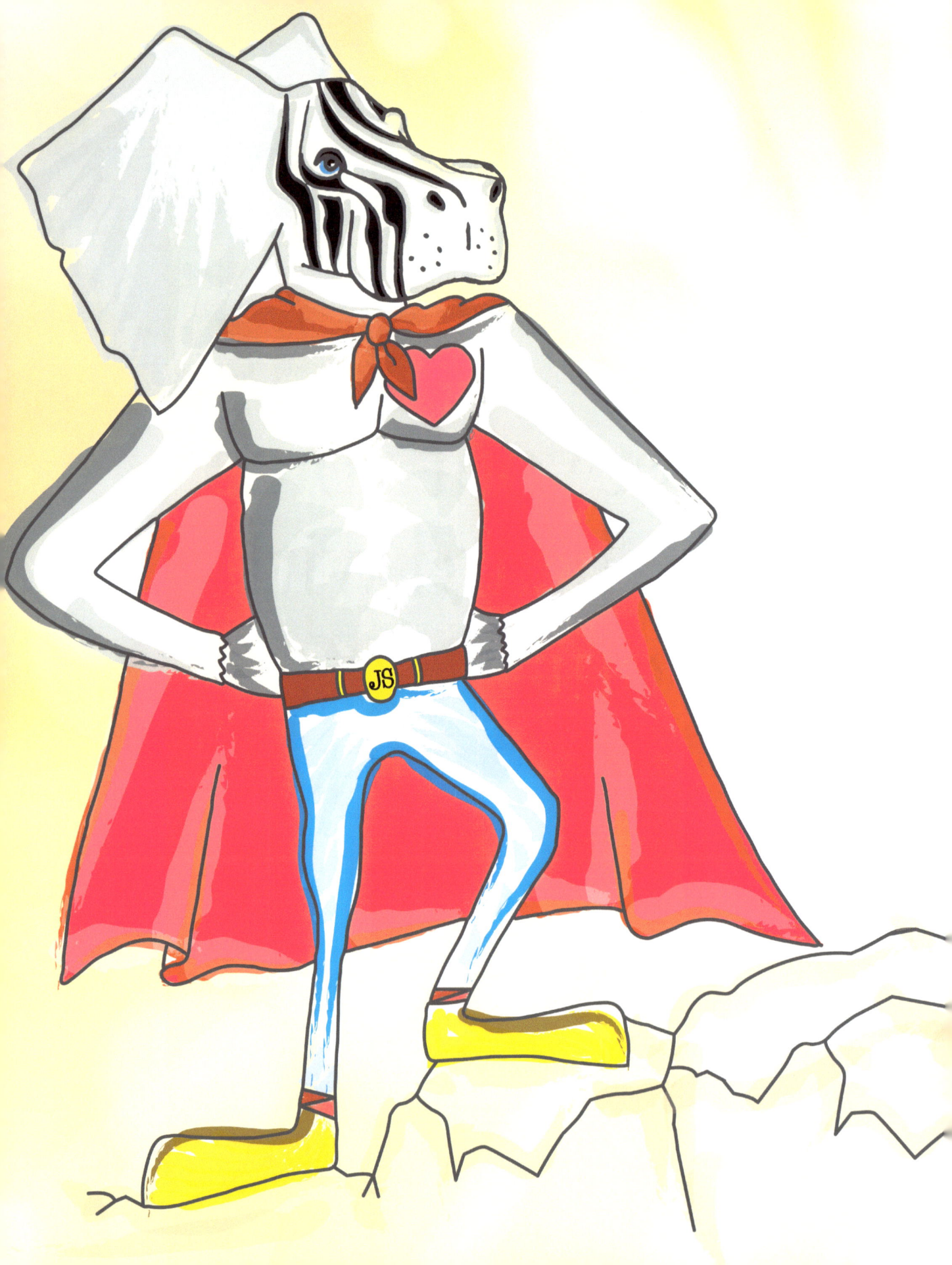

and know that
your super
zebra stripes
are one of a kind.

There is
only one

you in super.

www.ingramcontent.com/pod-product-compliance
Lightning Source LLC
Chambersburg PA
CBHW041003170626
46815CB00002B/142